for nathan and gordon
at christmas 1976
and for
  flying
    freeing
      and other
        special powers
          ♡
        Diane. joan

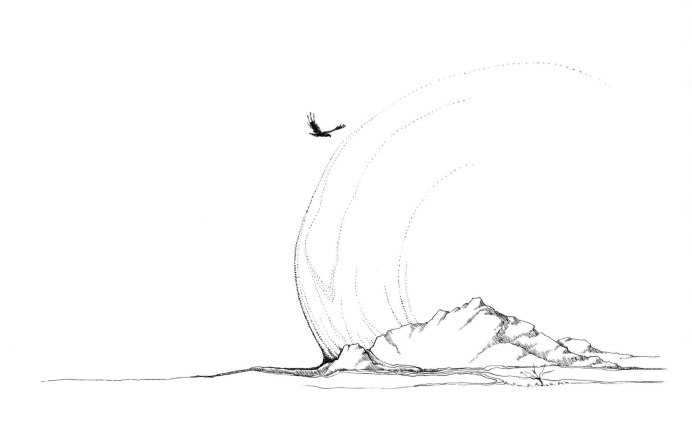

HAWK, I'M YOUR BROTHER

by BYRD BAYLOR
illustrated by PETER PARNALL

CHARLES SCRIBNER'S SONS | NEW YORK

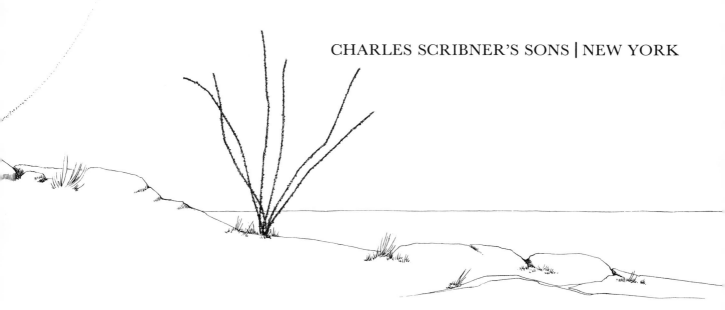

For Tony Schweitzer
and Charlie Ingram
because they both know about flying

Rudy Soto
dreams
of flying . . .

wants
to float
on the wind,
wants
to soar
over canyons.

He doesn't see himself
some little
light-winged bird
that flaps
and flutters
when it flies.
No cactus wren.
No sparrow.

He'd be
more like
a HAWK

gliding

smoother
than anything else
in the world.

He sees himself
a hawk
wrapped up in wind

lifting

facing the sun.

That's how
he wants
to fly.

That's all
he wants—
the only wish
he's ever had.

No matter what happens
he won't give it up.
He won't trade it
for easier wishes.

There,
playing alone
on the mountainside,
a dark skinny boy
calling out
to a hawk . . .

That's Rudy Soto.

People here say
that the day he was born
he looked at the sky
and lifted his hands
toward birds
and seemed to smile
at Santos Mountain.

The first words
he ever learned
were the words for
FLYING
and for
BIRD
and for
UP THERE . . . UP THERE.

And later on
they say that
every day
he asked his father,
"When do I learn to fly?"

 (He was too young then
to know
he'd never get his wish.)

His father said,
"You run.
You climb over rocks.
You jump around like a crazy
whirlwind.
Why do you need to fly?"

"I just do.
I need to fly."

In those days
he thought that
somebody
would give him
the answer.
He asked
everybody . . .

everybody.

And they always said,
"People don't fly."

"Never?"

"Never."

But Rudy Soto
told them this:
"*Some* people do.
Maybe we just don't know
those people.
Maybe they live
far away from here."

And when he met new people
he would
look at them
carefully.

"Can you fly?"

They'd only laugh
and shake their heads.

Finally he learned
to stop
asking.

Still,
he thought
that maybe
flying
is the secret
old people
keep
to themselves.
Maybe they go sailing
quietly
through the sky
when children
are asleep.

Or maybe
flying
is for
magic people.

And he even thought
that if no one else
in the world
could fly
he'd be the one
who would learn it.

"Somebody ought to,"
he said.
"Somebody.
Me!
Rudy Soto."

There,
barefoot
on the mountainside,
he'd
almost
fly.

He'd dream
he knew
the power
of great wings
and sing
up to the sun.

In his mind
he always seemed
to be a hawk,
the way he flew.

Of course
a boy like that
would know
every nest
this side of the mountain.
He'd know the time
in summer
when the young hawks
learn to fly.
And he'd think
a thousand times,
"Hawk, I'm your
brother.
Why am I stuck
down here?"

You have to know all this
to forgive the boy
for what he did.

And even then
you may not think
that he was right
to steal the bird.
It may seem
cruel
and selfish
and mean —
not worthy of one

who says
he's brother
to all birds.

But anyway
that's what he did.

He stole
a hawk —
a redtail hawk —
out of its nest
before the bird
could fly.

It was a nest
that Rudy Soto
must have seen
all his life,
high on the ledge
of a steep rough
canyon wall.

He thought
that nest
might be
the best home
in the world,
up there
on Santos Mountain.

And he even thought
that there might be
some special
magic
in a bird
that came from
Santos Mountain.

Somehow
he thought
he'd share
that
magic

and he'd *fly*.

They say
it used to
be
that way
when
we
knew how
to
talk
to birds

and how
to call
a bird's
wild spirit
down
into our own.

He'd heard
all those
old stories

and he'd seen
hawks
go flying
over mountains
and felt
their power
fill the sky.

It seemed to him
he'd FLY —

if
a hawk
became
his
brother.

That's why
he climbed
the cliff
at dawn
singing . . .

to make
the magic
stronger.

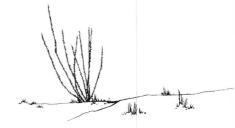

And
that's why
he left
an offering
of food . . .

to show
he was
that
brother.

But
the young hawk
struggled
and screamed,
called
to the birds
circling
overhead,
called
to its nest
on Santos Mountain.

"Listen, bird.
Don't be afraid.
Don't be
afraid
of *me*."

Climbing down,
he held
that bird
so close
he felt
its heartbeat
and
the bird
felt his.

"You'll be
all right.
You'll see."

But even a hawk
too young to fly
knows
he's meant
to fly.
He knows
he isn't meant
to have
a string
tied
to his leg.

He knows
he isn't meant
to live
in a cage.

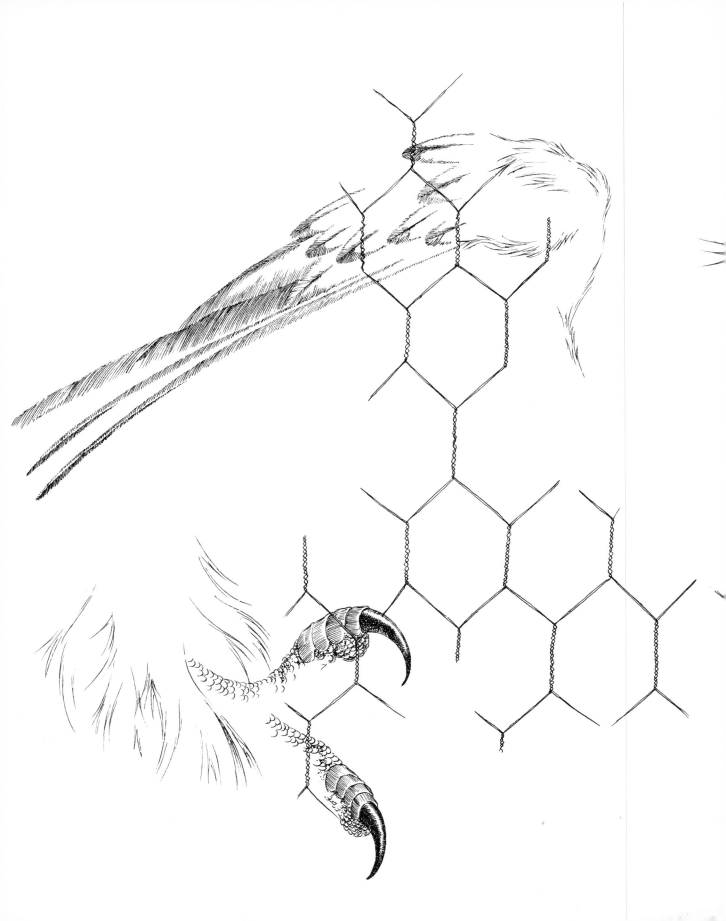

Every day
he screams.
He pulls
against the string.
He beats
his wings
against the cage.

"You'll be happy
with me, bird.
You will."

But the bird
looks out
with fierce
free
eyes
and calls
to its brothers
in the canyon.

Every day
it is the same.

They see
those
other birds
learning
to fly,
learning
the touch
and roll
and lift
of air,
learning
to
dip
and dive.
They turn
when
the wind
turns.

But
down below
with his feet
touching
sand
Rudy Soto's hawk
can only
flap
his wings
and rise
as high
as a string
will let him go.

Not high
enough.

Not far
enough.

Rudy Soto
tells his hawk:
"Someday
we'll fly
together."

He wants
to please
that hawk.
He's sure
he will.
He's sure
it's going to be
his
brother.

Each day
when the melons
are picked
and the wood
is chopped
and the corn
is hoed

Rudy Soto gives
a long soft call
and he comes
running.

He always says:
"I'm here now,
bird.
What do you want
to do?"

He takes the bird
out of the cage
and ties the string
around its foot
and the bird sits
on his shoulder
as they walk
the desert hills.

They go down
sandy washes
and
follow
deer tracks
into canyons.

Sometimes
they sit
looking off
to
Santos Mountain.

And sometimes
they even go
on the other side
of Santos Mountain
to a place
where
water
trickles
over
flat
smooth
rocks.

The bird
plays
in that
cold water . . .
dips
his wings
into the stream
and jumps
and flaps

and the boy says,
"See.
You're happy
here with me."

But
even
when he says it
he knows
it isn't true
because
the bird
is tugging
at the string

and
you see
sky
reflected in his eyes

and his eyes
flash

and his wings
move
with the
wind.

You can tell
he
wants
to
fly.

You can tell
that's
all

he wants,
the only
dream
he has.

Rudy Soto
knows
what
it is like
to want
to
fly.

He knows
himself
what
it is like
to have
a dream.

But even so
he waits
until
the end of summer,
hoping
that
the bird
will be
content.

Every day
it is the same.

The bird
still
tugs
and pulls
and yearns
against the string.

Rudy Soto
knows
that the hawk
will not
give up.

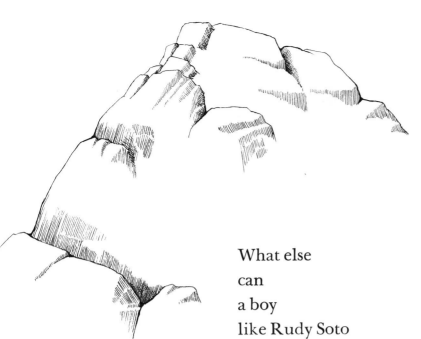

What else
can
a boy
like Rudy Soto
do?

He has to say:
"I don't want
to see you
so unhappy,
bird."

And he has to say:
"*One* of us
might as well
fly!"

What else
can he
do

if he
really
loves
that bird?

He has to
take him
back
to Santos Mountain
to the place
where *he*
would like
to fly.

That's where
they go —

up
to those
high
red rocks.

There is
a wind
and
clouds move
across
the sky
and
from far away
you can smell
rain.

Now he
unties
the string
that has held
his hawk
so
long.

The hawk
is on his
shoulder.

"Fly now,
bird.
Go on."

The hawk
turns.
He moves
his wings.

"Bird,
you can
fly."

The hawk
takes
his
time.

There
on the rocks
he jumps
and
flaps,

rises

and
sinks.

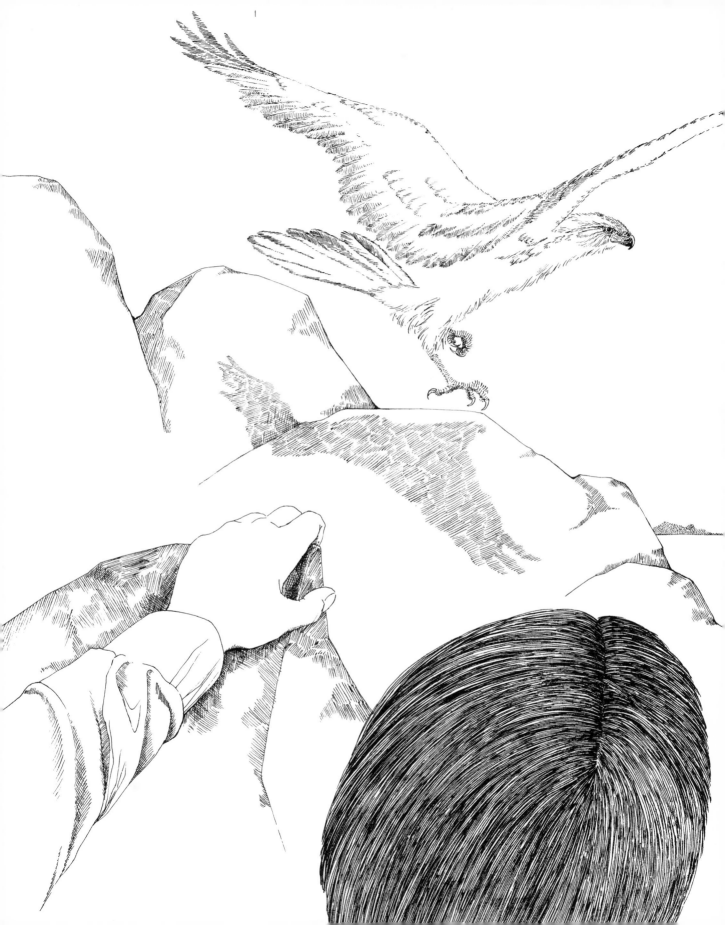

He
has
to learn
the force
of air
and the pull
of wind
and the feel
of
freedom.

Maybe
he jumps
a hundred times
before
he seems
to catch
the wind,
before
he lifts
himself
into
that
summer sky.

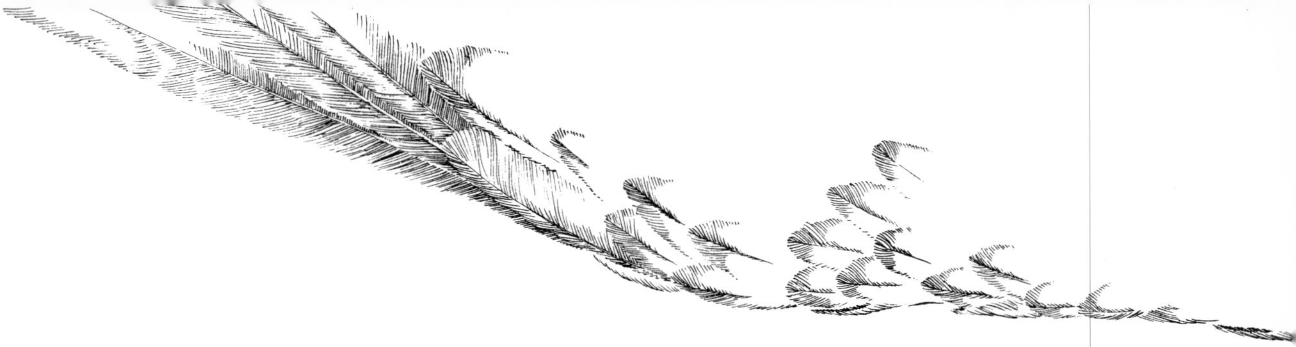

At last
he
soars.

His wings
shine
in the sun

and
the way
he
flies
is the way
Rudy Soto
always
dreamed
he'd fly.

The bird
looks
down.

Then
he calls
a long
hawk cry,
the kind of cry
he used to call
to his
brothers.

Only
this time
he calls
to
Rudy Soto

and the sound
floats
on the wind.

Rudy Soto
answers
with
the same
hawk
sound.

Back and forth
they call.

Brother
to
brother
they call

all through
the afternoon.

High
on the side
of Santos Mountain
Rudy Soto
lifts
his arms.
His hair
blows
in the wind
and
in his mind

he's
FLYING
too.

It doesn't
even matter
that
his feet
are on the
ground.

It seems to him
he has
the whole sky
to fly in

when
he hears
that
call.

He knows
he'll keep it
in his mind
forever.

Rudy Soto
doesn't tell
anybody.

He doesn't say:
"Lucky me.
I know
about
flying.
I know
about
wind."

He never says,
"There is a hawk
that is
my brother
so I have
a special
power."

But
people here
can tell
such things.

They notice
that a hawk
calls to him
from
Santos Mountain

and they hear
the way
he answers.

They see
that Rudy Soto
has a
different look
about him.

His eyes
flash
like
a young
hawk's
eyes

and there is
sky
reflected
in those eyes

and it's
the sky
high
over
Santos Mountain.

People here
are not
surprised.

They're
wise enough
to
understand
such things.

BYRD BAYLOR is the author of many distinguished books for children, two of which have been named Caldecott Honor Books—*When Clay Sings,* illustrated by Tom Bahti, and *The Desert Is Theirs,* illustrated by Peter Parnall. Among her other outstanding books are *They Put on Masks,* illustrated by Jerry Ingram, and *Everybody Needs a Rock,* illustrated by Peter Parnall, an ALA Notable book.

PETER PARNALL is one of the foremost illustrators in the country. His work has appeared in *Audubon Magazine* and *Scientific American,* as well as in many beautiful children's books. Of his most recent collaboration with Ms. Baylor, *The Desert Is Theirs, Horn Book* stated ". . . a unique, multi-dimensional presentation [that] is eloquent, profound, and totally absorbing."